MANAGING ANXIETY IN CHILDREN

A Comprehensive Guide for Parents and Caregivers

Helen J. Vogt

Managing Anxiety in Children

TABLE OF CONTENT

INTRODUCTION

Having recently relocated to a new city with her 6-year-old daughter Lily, Emily was a single mother. Emily had always been anxious, and she realized that Lily was beginning to show anxiety symptoms as well. When they had to leave the house, Lily would frequently sob and clutch to Emily and struggle to fall asleep at night.

Emily was aware that something needed to be done to assist Lily in controlling her anxiety, but she wasn't sure where to begin. When she was looking for information online, she came across a thorough guide for parents and caregivers for children with anxiety. She bought the book right away and started reading it from cover to cover.

Emily thought she had found a lifeline as she read. The manual included a wealth of doable tactics and research-proven treatments for controlling children's anxiety. She understood the value of providing Lily with a quiet and orderly atmosphere, and she put some of the advice for encouraging emotional control and resilience in her daughter into practice.

The case studies in the guide were also consoling to Emily. She realized that other parents had had similar challenges and had been successful in assisting their kids with anxiety management. As her daughter's conduct started to improve, she grew more confident in her abilities to support Lily.

Encouragement of Lily to employ coping mechanisms when she felt anxious was one of the techniques in the book that Emily found to be especially beneficial. Together, they practiced deep breathing, and Emily showed Lily how to picture a happy scene in her head. Along with doing yoga with her mother, Lily found that it was a great way to unwind and let go.

The manual also assisted Emily in understanding the significance of caregivers' self-care. She started to put more emphasis on her personal wellbeing, scheduling rest and exercise. She discovered that she was better able to assist Lily in controlling her anxiety as she become more composed and focused.

Emily was appreciative of the thorough guide and how it had improved her and Lily's lives. She shared the book with other parents in her neighborhood and felt as though she had discovered a caring group of people who were all attempting to assist their kids manage their anxiety.

Emily and Lily were able to work through their nervousness together and find peace and tranquility in their new city thanks to the advice and techniques in the guide.

For parents and other caregivers, controlling a child's anxiety can be a challenging undertaking. Although anxiety is a natural human feeling, it can become burdensome for both the kid and the caregiver when it manifests in overly severe ways and interferes with regular activities. The goal of this book is to give parents and other adults who care for children useful advice on how to help them manage their anxiety, develop resilience, and live healthy, happy lives. We will look at the various types of anxiety, their causes, and symptoms in this book, as well as provide evidence-based therapies to help kids manage their anxiety.

Nothing would make us happier as parents and caregivers than to watch our kids grow up confident, healthy, and happy. But the truth is that a lot of kids these days are dealing with anxiety. A child's ability to study, play, and interact with others can be significantly impacted by anxiety, whether it is caused by separation anxiety, social anxiety, or generalized anxiety disorder.

The book Managing Anxiety in Children: A Comprehensive Guide for Parents and Caregivers is a useful tool for anyone looking for doable tactics and research-proven treatments to assist kids in controlling their worry. The goal of this book is to serve as a thorough reference that addresses every aspect of childhood anxiety, including the many forms of anxiety, warning signs, and effective coping mechanisms.

You will discover how to support kids with various personalities and learning styles, as well as age-appropriate tactics for controlling anxiety, from toddlers to teenagers, through this guide. You will learn how family dynamics and parental upbringing can affect a child's anxiety as well as how to foster a supportive environment at home so that your child can better control their anxiety.

Every chapter will include evidence-based interventions, helpful advice, and case stories to demonstrate the various approaches that have been shown to be successful in reducing anxiety in young people. Our mission is to equip parents and other caregivers with the information and resources they need to support their anxious children and help them thrive.

Managing Anxiety in Children: A Comprehensive Guide for Parents and Caregivers is an invaluable tool that will assist you in comprehending and managing anxiety in children, whether you are a parent, grandparent, teacher, or other caregiver. You can encourage your children to develop resilience and have happy, meaningful lives by actively participating in their mental health and wellbeing.

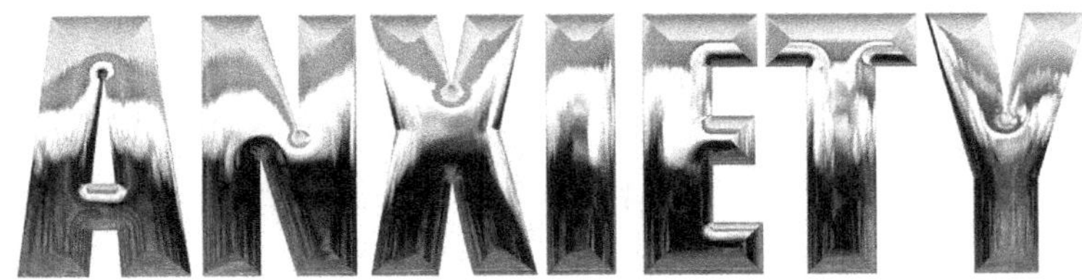

Managing Anxiety in Children

CHAPTER 1

Understanding Children's Anxiety

Anxiety is a typical aspect of childhood and is a natural reaction to stress or danger. A child's daily life and growth may be hampered by anxiety, though, if it is excessive and chronic. This chapter will cover the definition of anxiety as well as the different forms of pediatric anxiety disorders, its causes, symptoms, and indicators.

The meaning of anxiety

A sensation of unease, fear, or worry is known as anxiety. It is a typical reaction to stress or danger and can assist a child get ready for a tough or unpleasant scenario. A child's daily life and growth may be hampered by anxiety, though, if it is excessive and chronic. Different symptoms of anxiety might appear, including behavioral, emotional, and physical symptoms.

Types of Anxiety Disorders in Children

The most prevalent mental health conditions in children are anxiety disorders. Anxiety problems impact 1 in 8 children, according to the American Academy of Child and Adolescent Psychiatry. The following list includes some of the most typical types of anxiety disorders in kids:

Disorder of Separation Anxiety

Excessive stress and anxiety about being apart from a parent or caregiver are characteristics of this form of anxiety disorder. Children with separation anxiety disorder cannot want to go to school or other activities, feel physical symptoms like headaches or stomachaches, and have nightmares about being separated.

Case Study: When Samantha, a 7-year-old girl, is dropped off at school by her mother each morning, she sobs. Samantha frequently begs her mother to stay with her, and if she does, Samantha gets frustrated and won't participate in class. Samantha is a good student, according to her teacher, when she is able to stay in class, but her anxiety is beginning to lower her grades.

Disorder of Social Anxiety

Children with social anxiety disorder may avoid social situations altogether due to their severe dread of them. They can worry about saying or doing the wrong thing and fear being criticized or embarrassed. This may result in social isolation and friendship difficulties.

Case Study: Ten-year-old Adam has always been reserved. He finds it difficult to speak up in class or take part in team activities. When his parents ask him why he never wants to host guests or go to social gatherings, he becomes noticeably nervous and claims that he is terrified of being judged or making a mistake.

Specific phobia

Specific phobias are extreme, unreasonable fears about certain things or circumstances. A young person might, for instance, fear dogs or spiders. These crippling anxieties may lead kids to shun specific locations or activities.

Case Study: Six-year-old Jenny suffers from a terrible phobia of dogs. Every time she sees a dog, she feels incredibly worried and terrified, and if one approaches too closely, she will wail or scream. Her parents have observed that her dread has grown so strong that she no longer leaves the house out of concern that she could run into a dog outside.

Disorder of Generalized Anxiety

Children who have generalized anxiety disorder worry and fear too much about a wide range of things, and they may also experience physical symptoms like muscle tightness or trouble sleeping. Since the fears are frequently nebulous and hard to specify, this sort of anxiety disorder can be challenging to diagnose.

Jacob, an eight-year-old child, is a worrier about everything. In an effort to get assurance that everything will be alright, he frequently asks his parents the same questions over and time again. He struggles to fall asleep at night and frequently whines about stomachaches. His parents are worried that his worry prevents him from taking pleasure in normal childhood activities.

Readers can gain a better understanding of how anxiety can appear in children and the effects it can have on their life by offering case studies or brief anecdotes that exemplify each form of anxiety condition.

Causes of Anxiety in Children

There are many different things that might make a child anxious, including their genes, brain chemistry, temperament, past experiences, and the environment. Genetics, brain chemistry, or temperament may all play a role in why some kids are more prone to worry than others. Some kids might, for instance, be innately anxious or more susceptible to stress. Events in life, such as trauma, abuse, or bereavement, can also cause or make children more anxious. Environmental elements like family strife, academic stress, or social demands can further exacerbate children's anxiety.

Children's Anxiety Symptoms and Signs

Many children experience anxiety, a common mental health issue. In order to provide their charges the support and assistance they require, parents and other caregivers must be able to identify the warning signs and symptoms of anxiety in children.

Depending on the child's age, personality, and the type of anxiety illness they are suffering, the signs and symptoms of anxiety in children might change. However, a few widespread symptoms and indicators include:

- **Overwhelming fear and worry:** Children with anxiety disorders may experience overwhelming fear and worry over regular occurrences like going to school, making friends, or being away from their parents. They might also have unreasonable phobias like a fear of the dark or a dread of being by themselves.

- **Physical symptoms:** Children who experience anxiety may experience stomachaches, headaches, dizziness, and nausea.

- **Sleep disturbances:** Children with anxiety disorders may experience nightmares or night terrors, as well as difficulty getting asleep or staying asleep.

- **Avoidance actions:** Anxious children may steer clear of circumstances or behaviors that make them feel anxious, such as attending school, interacting with peers, or taking part in extracurricular activities.

- **Irritability:** Children may become more irritable or easily disturbed when they are anxious, which can result in tantrums or other outbursts.

It's crucial to remember that similar symptoms may occur in kids without anxiety disorders and that some anxiety is common in kids. However, if these symptoms persist and affect the child's ability to go about their daily lives, it may be an indication of an anxiety problem.

Parents and other caregivers should pay close attention to their child's behavior and mood and be open to discussing their thoughts and anxieties with them in order to recognize these signs and symptoms early. It's also crucial to get professional assistance if the symptoms increase or persist because therapy and, in some situations, medicines are effective treatments for anxiety disorders.

It is crucial to remember that not all anxious kids may exhibit the same symptoms, and some kids may have more subdued or internalized signs and symptoms.

CHAPTER TWO

Effects of anxiety on kids

In children, anxiety is a frequent mental health issue that, if ignored, can negatively affect both their development and general wellbeing. We will talk about how anxiety impacts a child's growth, academic achievement, and physical health in this chapter.

How anxiety impacts a child's growth and general wellbeing

Anxiety can significantly affect a child's growth and general wellbeing. Children who struggle with anxiety may find it difficult to interact with others, which lower their confidence and self-esteem. Fear and worry may also prevent them from making friends or taking part in new activities.

A child's emotional growth may be hampered by anxiety, which can result in emotions like grief, rage, and frustration. They may struggle with emotional regulation and have difficulties managing their emotions. Additionally, anxiety can hinder a child's cognitive growth, impairing their ability to pay attention, recall information, and solve issues.

Additionally, anxiety can have an impact on a child's physical well-being by causing signs and symptoms including tension headaches, nausea, and stomachaches. Children who struggle with anxiety may often have trouble falling asleep, which can cause further health issues.

How anxiety affects a kid's academic performance

The effects of anxiety on a child's academic achievement can be profound. Children who battle with anxiety may have problems attending school on a regular basis and may find it difficult to concentrate and finish their work. Additionally, anxiety can hinder a child's capacity to learn, which can cause problems in math, reading, and writing.

Children who deal with anxiety may also have trouble taking tests, which can result in subpar grades and a decline in academic confidence. In some circumstances, anxiety might cause a youngster to avoid going to school because of worry and fear.

Relationship between physical health and anxiety

A child's physical health can be significantly impacted by anxiety. Many other physical symptoms, such as headaches, stomachaches, tension in the muscles, and exhaustion, can be present in children with anxiety. They might also have sleep issues, which could cause additional health issues.

Additionally, anxiety can weaken a child's immune system and increase their susceptibility to infections like the flu and the common cold. Long-term health issues including high blood pressure and heart disease can also result from chronic anxiety.

Recognizing the symptoms and indicators of anxiety in kids

To give children the necessary support and therapy, parents and other caregivers must be able to recognize the telltale signs and symptoms of anxiety. Excessive worry or fear about regular occurrences or activities; refusal to attend school or participate in social situations; trouble sleeping or recurring nightmares; physical symptoms like headaches, stomachaches, and muscle tension; irritability, mood swings, or emotional outbursts; avoidance of new activities or situations; difficulty concentrating or finishing tasks; and excessive reassurance.

It is critical to get professional assistance from a mental health expert or healthcare practitioner if you detect any of these behaviors or indications in your child. The long-term effects of anxiety on a child's development and well-being can be reduced with early intervention and treatment.

Anxiety Medicine

CHAPTER THREE

Parental Training and Children's Anxiety

Promoting emotional growth and controlling children's conduct are just two of the many obligations that come with being a parent, which is a difficult and complex responsibility. It is crucial to realize that a child's emotional development, including the emergence of anxiety, is greatly influenced by the parenting style of the parent. Parents have the power to encourage emotional regulation in kids, resilience in kids, and general wellbeing in kids. This chapter will examine how parental parenting affects children's anxiety development and offer techniques for fostering emotional control and resilience.

Parents' Influence on Children's Emotional Development

When it comes to a child's emotional growth, including the emergence of anxiety, parents play a critical influence. A child's ability to regulate their emotions and develop coping mechanisms can be influenced by the way parents engage with them, the strength of their bond with them, and the parenting approach taken. Children who are raised in homes where their parents' love, support, and encouragement are felt are more likely to be emotionally stable and resilient.

In contrast, children who encounter neglect, abuse, or inconsistent parenting as they grow up are more likely to experience anxiety and other mental health problems. Children tend to acquire stronger emotional regulation and coping mechanisms when their parents show them warmth, affection, and emotional support.

Methods to Aid Parents in Fostering Children's Emotional Control and Resilience

Parents can use a variety of techniques to encourage their kids' emotional control and resilience. These consist of:

- **Fostering emotional expression:** Parents can support their kids' emotional expression by giving them a secure environment. This can be accomplished through parents listening to their kids, validating their feelings, and offering assistance when required.

- **Fostering analytical thinking:** By encouraging their kids to solve their own problems, parents can aid in the development of these talents in their kids. This can be accomplished by giving advice and encouragement while letting their kids make their own judgments.

- **Teaching coping mechanisms:** To help their kids manage their emotions and anxieties, parents can teach their kids coping mechanisms like relaxation methods, encouraging self-talk, and mindfulness.

Parents can encourage good habits such as frequent exercise, a nutritious diet, and sufficient sleep, all of which can improve a child's ability to regulate their emotions and overall wellbeing.

Common Parenting Practices That May Increase Children's Anxiety

Numerous prevalent parenting philosophies could make kids more anxious. These parenting philosophies may have an impact on a child's emotional growth and capacity to handle stress. Here are some instances of how various parenting philosophies might make kids more anxious:

Overly cautious parenting (overprotective)

This parenting approach is becoming extremely involved in a child's life to the point of limiting and regulating it. Parents who are overly protective may prevent their kids from taking risks or facing obstacles, which may limit their capacity to grow in coping mechanisms and resilience. Anxiety can develop in children of overprotective parents when they face obstacles or unexpected settings.

Dictatorial Parenting

There are little opportunities for compromise or negotiation in this parenting approach, which entails tight rules and discipline. Authoritarian parents may employ punishment as a form of management, which can result in a stressful and tense atmosphere at home. When they believe they have no control over their life or when they make mistakes, children of authoritarian parents may experience anxiety.

Lenient Parenting (permissive)

This parenting approach places less emphasis on structure and regulations, instead letting kids do what they want. Conflict may be avoided and repercussions for misconduct may not be enforced by permissive parents. Children may experience an unstable and unpredictable environment as a result, which may increase anxiety. When confronted with circumstances that call for boundaries or structure, children of permissive parents may experience anxiety.

Stern Parenting (critical)

High expectations and ongoing criticism of a child's actions and accomplishments are characteristics of this parenting approach. Children who have critical parents may be constantly reminded of their flaws, which can lead to feelings of inadequacy and low self-esteem. When they believe they are not living up to expectations or when they make mistakes, children of critical parents may experience anxiety.

It's crucial to understand that many parents may combine different parenting approaches, as they are not mutually incompatible. Furthermore, it's crucial to understand that various parenting philosophies might cause anxiety when used excessively or unbalanced, but they are not always wrong or harmful.

It's critical for parents to be aware of their own parenting behaviors and how they might be affecting their kids' emotional growth. It is possible to build emotional control and resilience in your child by attempting to strike a balance between structure, support, and encouragement. If you think your parenting style is causing your child's anxiety, it's also crucial to get help and advice.

The emotional development of a kid, including the emergence of anxiety, is greatly influenced by parental upbringing. By employing a variety of techniques, including emotional expression, the teaching of problem-solving techniques, the teaching of coping mechanisms, and the promotion of healthy behaviors, parents can help their children develop emotional regulation and resilience. To encourage their children's emotional resilience and well-being, parents should work to create a supportive, caring, and nurturing atmosphere.

CHAPTER FOUR

Child Anxiety Management Techniques

Although anxiety is a normal aspect of human growth, it can become troublesome if it gets out of control or starts to interfere with regular tasks. Fortunately, there are various evidence-based therapies and coping methods that can be beneficial in reducing anxiety in children. In this chapter, we'll go over a few of these techniques and how parents and other adults can help kids manage their anxiety.

Evidence-Based Strategies for Treating Children's Anxiety

CBT or cognitive behavioral therapy

A well-known evidence-based technique for reducing anxiety in children is cognitive-behavioral therapy (CBT). CBT teaches kids how to recognize and combat the unfavorable attitudes, beliefs, and thoughts that fuel their fear. Children who receive therapy also acquire coping mechanisms to control their worried thoughts and actions.

Interventions Based on Mindfulness

Children's anxiety has also been proven to be successfully managed by mindfulness-based interventions like mindfulness-based stress reduction (MBSR) and mindfulness-based cognitive therapy (MBCT). The impact of worried thoughts and feelings can be lessened by using mindfulness techniques on kids.

Explicit Therapy

Another evidence-based strategy for treating children's anxiety is exposure therapy. In a safe and encouraging setting, exposure therapy entails gradually exposing kids to events they are afraid of. This can lessen the intensity and frequency of anxious feelings in kids as well as provide them a sense of control over their worry.

Managing Anxiety in Children

Coping mechanisms that kids can employ when they're anxious

Children can employ a variety of coping mechanisms in addition to evidence-based therapy when they are experiencing nervous. Among these coping mechanisms are:

- **Deep Inhalation:** When kids are feeling stressed, deep breathing is a quick and efficient method to help them calm down. Encourage your kid to breathe deeply and slowly, using their nose for inhalation and their mouth for exhalation.

- **Progressively Relaxing the Muscles:** To relieve tension in the muscles and encourage relaxation, different muscle groups are tense and relaxed successively. Children who feel the physical signs of anxiety, such as headaches and muscle tension, may find this therapy beneficial.

- **Positivity in Oneself:** Teach your youngster to confront unfavorable attitudes and beliefs by talking positively to themselves. Encourage them to think only positive thoughts and to constantly remind themselves of their qualities and strengths.

How to Support Children in Managing Their Anxiety as Parents and Caregivers

Additionally, there are a number of techniques that parents and other adults can employ to help kids manage their anxiety. Some of these tactics consist of:

- **Giving emotional assistance:** It's crucial for parents and other adults to offer children who are anxious emotional assistance. As you are listening to your child's worries, reassure and support them.

- **Modeling Effective Coping Techniques:** Positive coping techniques like deep breathing and encouraging self-talk can be modeled by parents and other caregivers. This can teach kids good anxiety management techniques.

- **Making a Friendly Environment:** Children's anxiety can also be managed by creating a supportive atmosphere. This entails establishing a regular schedule with clear expectations and boundaries as well as a secure and comforting home environment.

Although managing children's anxiety can be difficult, there are a number of evidence-based therapies and coping mechanisms that can be useful in easing anxiety symptoms. In addition, by offering emotional support, demonstrating effective coping mechanisms, and fostering a supportive atmosphere, parents and other adults can play a significant part in helping kids manage their anxiety.

CHAPTER FIVE

Developing Children's Resilience

The capacity to cope with stress and adversity and to recover from trying situations is known as resilience. In children, resilience is particularly important because it can help them cope with the obstacles and stressors that they unavoidably meet as they grow and develop.

Various tactics can be used to foster children's resilience and give them the tools and resources they need to overcome challenges and prosper. Some of these tactics consist of:

- **Fostering fruitful connections:** Resilience is more likely to develop in children who have supportive and caring interactions with their parents, carers and other adults. These connections give youngsters a sense of stability and security as well as a sense of worth and love.

- **Promoting creative problem-solving:** Children who master these skills are better prepared to face difficulties and conquer hurdles. Parents and other adults who provide care for children can encourage them by applauding their perseverance and encouraging them to investigate other solutions to challenges.

- **Fostering autonomy and independence:** Children who are allowed to take on age-appropriate duties and make their own decisions gain self-efficacy and a sense of confidence that can help them face problems. Giving children the freedom to make decisions and take on chores while also offering them the necessary support and direction can help kids develop independence.

- **Encouraging positive self-talk:** Encourage children to adopt positive self-talk so they can handle stress and adversity better. Parents and other adult caregivers can support children by encouraging them to replace negative thoughts with positive ones and by setting an example of good self-talk.

- **Teaching coping mechanisms:** Children who possess a variety of coping mechanisms are more capable of managing stress and anxiety. Exercise, social support, and relaxation methods can all be used as coping mechanisms. Children can benefit from parents and other caregivers teaching them these techniques and encouraging them to apply them when they are stressed or anxious.

Children's capacity to control anxiety can benefit from the development of resilience. Children who are more resilient are better able to manage stress and anxiety and are more likely to recover from challenging situations.

In order to improve children's general wellbeing and provide them the tools and resources they need to deal with life's obstacles, it is crucial to help them develop their resilience. By developing healthy relationships, promoting problem-solving abilities, encouraging independence and autonomy, encouraging positive self-talk, and teaching coping mechanisms, parents and other caregivers can play a crucial part in fostering children's resilience. Children can become resilient individuals who are better able to handle life's ups and downs by being encouraged to be resilient as children.

Managing Anxiety in Children

CHAPTER SIX

Managing Anxiety in Different Personality Types

Every child is different, and they each have distinctive personality qualities that influence how they feel and handle worry. Understanding these personality types and how to support kids in managing their anxiety are crucial for parents and other caregivers.

The Obsessive

Perfectionists have a great desire to complete things flawlessly and are highly motivated. They frequently have high standards for themselves and when they don't live up to them, they could be extremely judgmental or nervous. By encouraging perfectionistic kids to set reasonable objectives and expectations as well as by teaching them to take pride in their accomplishments, parents and caregivers can help perfectionistic kids.

The Anxious

Managing Anxiety in Children

Worriers frequently experience anxiety over a variety of issues, from minor everyday worries to more significant, abstract dread. They may find it difficult to handle uncertainty or change, so techniques like mindfulness or cognitive-behavioral therapy may be helpful. Children who worry can benefit from their parents and other caregivers showing them how to recognize and combat negative thoughts as well as good coping mechanisms for stress and anxiety.

The Skipper

Avoiders tend to avoid anxiety-inducing situations and may experience problems with social anxiety or separation anxiety. By gradually introducing avoidant children to fearful circumstances in a safe and regulated way, as well as by praising and encouraging their efforts to face their anxieties, parents and caregivers can encourage avoidant children.

The Sensation-Seeker

When they do not get enough sensory input, such as movement, touch, or music, sensory-seekers may get anxious or agitated. To assist control their sensory needs, they may benefit from tactics like exercise, deep pressure massage, or fidget toys. Children who are sensory seekers can be helped by their parents and caregivers by giving them opportunities for sensory play and exploration and by teaching them self-control techniques.

The Shy Person

Children that are introverted may experience anxiety or overload in social settings and may benefit from techniques like role-playing or social storytelling to boost their confidence. Respecting their need for solitude and offering opportunity for calmer, more alone activities are two ways that parents and other adults can help introverted kids.

The Outgoing

Children that are extroverted may experience anxiety if they don't have enough stimulation or social connection. To aid in the formation of wholesome social bonds, they may profit from tactics like play dates, group activities, or social skills instruction. By giving extroverted kids the chance to interact with others, parents and other adults may assist them while also appreciating and respecting their need for rest and self-care.

Parents and other adults who care for children can better support them in controlling their anxiety and creating good coping mechanisms by recognizing the distinctive personality features that each child possesses.

CHAPTER SEVEN

The School's Function in Child Anxiety Management

A major part of a child's life is school, which for many kids may be stressful and anxiety-inducing. Schools must be aware of how common anxiety in children is and must have plans in place to help students who experience anxiety. In this chapter, we'll examine how schools can help kids manage their anxiety and talk about teaching methods that can help kids develop emotional control and resilience.

How Schools Can Help Anxious Children

Schools are essential in assisting kids with anxiety management. Schools may help kids feel safe, secure, and valued by fostering a supportive and nurturing environment. The following are a few methods that schools might assist students who are anxious:

- **Create Good Relationships:** Building trusting relationships with children might help them feel less anxious and more a part of the school community. Teachers and other members of the faculty can spend time getting to know each kid, demonstrating empathy, and offering assistance.

- **Create a Safe and Encouragement Environment:** By implementing procedures and policies that support emotional health, educational institutions can foster a secure and encouraging atmosphere. A clear anti-bullying policy, encouraging good behavior, and facilitating access to mental health resources are a few examples of how to do this.

- **Use interventions with evidence:** Children who experience anxiety can benefit from evidence-based interventions including cognitive behavioral therapy and mindfulness. Schools and mental health specialists can collaborate to offer these interventions to pupils who require them.

- **Develop a growth mentality:** A growth mindset emphasizes the notion that intelligence and skills can be improved through perseverance and hard work. Schools can encourage a growth mindset by encouraging effort and tenacity, recognizing progress rather than just accomplishment, and giving kids chances to succeed despite failure.

Techniques for Teachers and School Staff to Encourage Children's Emotional Control and Resilience

In addition to the aforementioned, teachers and other school personnel can employ particular techniques to encourage children's emotional control and resilience. Here are a few instances:

- **Teaching Coping Techniques**: Teachers can instruct their pupils in coping mechanisms including deep breathing, mindfulness, and encouraging self-talk. Children who struggle to control their emotions and cope with worry may benefit from these techniques.

- **Encourage Physical Activity:** Studies have proven that physical activity improves mental wellness. Teachers can encourage pupils to engage in physical activity by incorporating movement breaks into the school day.

- **Develop Social and Emotional Skills:** Anxiety management requires social-emotional abilities like empathy, self-awareness, and self-control. These abilities can be taught by teachers via exercises like role-playing, group discussions, and journaling.

- **Create a Structured atmosphere:** A structured atmosphere is typically beneficial for children who are anxious. Teachers can help children feel more in control and less anxious by setting clear expectations, routines, and schedules.

Schools are crucial in helping youngsters manage their anxiety. Schools may support students in managing their anxiety and achieving academic and social success by providing a secure and encouraging atmosphere, implementing evidence-based interventions, and encouraging emotional control and resilience. By using these techniques, teachers and other school personnel can contribute to the development of a friendly and encouraging learning environment for kids who struggle with anxiety.

CHAPTER EIGHT

Age-Specific Methods of Controlling Anxiety

All ages can be affected by anxiety, and different age groups will require different management techniques. This chapter will cover age-appropriate methods for dealing with anxiety in young children, school-age children, and teenagers.

Preschoolers

Preschoolers often range in age from three to five. Children at this age may have trouble expressing their emotions since they are still working on their language and social abilities. Preschoolers that are anxious may cling to parents, cry a lot, throw temper tantrums, and have trouble falling asleep.

Play therapy is one efficient method for calming preschoolers' anxiety. In a secure and encouraging setting, play therapy enables kids to express their feelings and deal with their fear. Toys, puppets, and other playthings may be used by the therapist to assist the kid in exploring their emotions and acquiring coping mechanisms.

Using relaxation techniques is another method for reducing anxiety in preschoolers. To help young children relax and quiet down when they feel anxious, simple strategies can be taught, such as progressive muscle relaxation, deep breathing, and visualization.

School-aged Children

Children that are ready for school are normally between the ages of 6 and 12. Children are more able to articulate their feelings at this age, and they may also be more aware of the causes and consequences of anxiety. Children who are in school-age might experience anxiety in a variety of ways, including excessive worrying, trouble concentrating, avoiding social situations, and physical symptoms like headaches and stomachaches.

An effective evidence-based technique for treating anxiety in school-aged children is cognitive-behavioral therapy

(CBT). Children can identify and fight harmful attitudes and beliefs that fuel their anxiety with the use of CBT. To assist the child in creating coping mechanisms, the therapist may employ a number of treatments including exposure therapy, relaxation training, and problem-solving skills.

Along with treatment, parents and other caregivers can help school-age children by creating a secure atmosphere, promoting healthy behaviors like exercise and sleep, and instructing them in relaxation methods like deep breathing and mindfulness.

Teenagers

Teenagers usually range in age from 13 to 18 years old. Young people are going through major life changes at this age, including more demanding academic requirements, peer pressure, and changes to their bodies and relationships. Teenagers who are anxious may worry excessively, avoid social settings, become agitated, or have physical symptoms like headaches and stomachaches.

Teenage anxiety can be effectively managed with cognitive behavioral therapy. Furthermore, studies on this age group have indicated that mindfulness-based therapies are successful in lowering anxiety and enhancing general well-being. Through meditation and other practices, one can develop mindfulness, which is being open and non-judgmental while one pays attention to the moment.

By supporting healthy behaviors like exercise, sleep, and a balanced diet, parents and other caregivers may support teenagers who are anxious. They can also serve as role models for beneficial coping mechanisms like mindfulness and problem-solving techniques. Creating a secure and encouraging environment in which teenagers feel free to express their emotions and ask for assistance when necessary is also crucial.

Age-appropriate techniques that consider the child's developmental stage and unique requirements are necessary for managing anxiety in children. Children can build the resilience and coping mechanisms necessary to control their anxiety and thrive through a combination of counseling, relaxation techniques, and support from parents, caregivers, and schools.

CHAPTER NINE

Understanding Medication for Anxiety in Children

Understanding Medication for Children's Anxiety in Anxiety problems can significantly affect a child's functioning and overall well-being. To treat the symptoms of anxiety, medication may occasionally be advised. However, children's anxiety should never be treated with medication as a first option. Instead of resorting to medicine, it is crucial to take into account the child's particular needs and circumstances and to look into evidence-based interventions.

Types of Drugs Used to Treat Children's Anxiety

Many different sorts of drugs can be used to treat children's anxiety. These consist of:

- **Selective serotonin reuptake inhibitors (SSRIs):** These drugs are frequently prescribed to treat depression and anxiety disorders. They function by raising the brain's concentration of the neurotransmitter serotonin, which can elevate mood and lessen anxiety. Fluvoxamine (Luvox), sertraline (Zoloft), and fluoxetine (Prozac) are a few SSRIs that may be used to treat anxiety in kids.

- **Serotonin-norepinephrine reuptake inhibitors (SNRIs):** Medications known as serotonin-norepinephrine reuptake inhibitors (SNRIs) are also used to treat depression and anxiety disorders. They function by raising the brain's concentrations of serotonin and norepinephrine. Venlafaxine (Effexor) and duloxetine (Cymbalta) are two SNRIs that may be used to treat anxiety in young patients.

- **Benzodiazepines:** Despite the possibility of dependence and other negative effects, these drugs are typically only used as a last resort when treating anxiety in young patients. Benzodiazepines function by boosting the effects of GABA, a neurotransmitter that can help lessen anxiety. Alprazolam (Xanax) and diazepam (Valium) are two benzodiazepines that can be used to treat anxiety in kids.

Benefits and Risks of Medications Used to Treat Childhood Anxiety

Depending on the individual circumstances and needs of the kid, it may be appropriate to use medication to treat anxiety in children. The use of medicine to treat childhood anxiety carries both advantages and disadvantages.

Benefits of treating children's anxiety with medication include:

- **Reduced Signs of Anxiousness**: Medication can lessen the severity and frequency of anxiety symptoms, allowing kids to go about their daily lives more easily.

- **Higher Standard Of Living:** Medication can enhance a child's overall quality of life by easing anxiety symptoms and enabling them to participate in activities that they may have previously avoided because of their anxiety.

- **Enhanced efficiency of additional therapies:** Sometimes, medicine might help other treatments—like therapy—be more effective.

The following are risks of treating children's anxiety with medication:

All medications have the potential to have side effects, and some of the adverse reactions to treatments for anxiety can be very significant. Drowsiness, nausea, and headaches are typical adverse effects of anxiety drugs.

- **Dependence:** Some anxiety drugs have a habit-forming side effect that can result in dependence or addiction.
- **Possible long-term consequences:** Certain anxiety drugs may increase the risk of cognitive decline and other health issues later in life, according to some research, if they are used long-term.

When a Child with Anxiety May Benefit from Medication

The first line of treatment for anxiety in children should never be medication. Instead, it is preferable to start by looking into evidence-based interventions like cognitive-behavioral therapy and mindfulness. For a youngster with anxiety, medication might be necessary in some circumstances. Medication may be considered in the following circumstances:

- **When worry is intense:** Medication may be recommended if a child's anxiety is interfering with their daily life and they are unable to participate in activities that are age appropriate. Medication can help lessen the severity and frequency of these symptoms, which can be caused by severe anxiety and appear as physical symptoms like panic attacks.

- **When therapy for anxiety is ineffective:** Evidence-based therapies like cognitive-behavioral therapy or mindfulness may occasionally fail to help a child. In certain circumstances, therapy and medication may be combined to control anxiety.

- **When another condition coexists with anxiety:** When ADHD and depression co-occur in a child, medication may be administered to treat both illnesses. A skilled healthcare expert should prescribe medicine for anxiety, and it should be used in conjunction with therapy.

- **When a child's anxiety is affecting their physical health:** Physical symptoms like headaches, stomachaches, and trouble sleeping might be a sign of anxiety. In these situations, a drug may be provided to help the youngster control their anxiety and to relieve these symptoms.

The advantages and disadvantages of anxiety medication should be thoroughly discussed by parents and carers with their child's doctor. Only use medication under the supervision of a trained healthcare expert, and keep a close eye on its efficacy and any possible negative effects. It is also critical to remember that medicine should not be used as a stand-alone treatment for anxiety; rather, it should be used in conjunction with evidence-based therapies and parental and caregiver support.

CHAPTER TEN

Self-Care is Important for Caregivers

Taking care of an anxious child can be taxing and frustrating. It's crucial for caregivers to be aware of the effects their work may have on their own physical and emotional health. Maintaining your well-being is crucial, and practicing self-care can help you better assist and control your child's worry.

The Effects of Caregiving on the Mental and Physical Health of the Caregiver

Caregiving for an anxious child can provide a variety of mental and emotional difficulties. The strain and demands of this job may increase the likelihood of depression, anxiety, and other chronic illnesses, among other detrimental health effects. Along with stress about money and disturbances to their personal and professional lives, caregivers may also feel alone, guilty, and worn out.

Caregiver burnout, which is characterized by a condition of emotional, physical, and mental tiredness, may occur if sufficient self-care is not practiced. Detachment, cynicism, and a reduction in empathy for the child and those around them are all symptoms of burnout. It's critical for carers to understand the warning symptoms of burnout and take action to avoid it.

Self-care Techniques for Caregivers

Self-care is essential for preserving the physical and mental health of caregivers. Caregivers can support their own health and wellbeing in a variety of ways, including the following:

- **Take breaks:** It's critical that carers regularly get away from their caregiving duties. This can entail setting aside time to relax, engage in fun hobbies, and spend time with loved ones.

- **Prioritize sleep:** Putting sleep first to keep one's physical and mental health, one must get adequate sleep. Caregivers should strive to get 7-9 hours of sleep each night, and may need to adopt a consistent sleep regimen to ensure they are getting the rest they need.

- **Eat a balanced, nutritious diet:** Caregivers can improve their general health and energy levels by eating a diet that is both balanced and nutritious.

- **Exercise frequently:** Exercise frequently can help lower stress and improve general health and wellbeing. Even if it's only a quick stroll or some stretching, caregivers should make it a point to move around each day.

- **Seek assistance:** Because providing care might feel solitary, it's crucial for carers to enlist assistance from others. This can involve meeting with a therapist, joining a support group, or just chatting to close friends and relatives.

The link between caregiver self-care and controlling children's anxiety

The ability of parents to control their child's anxiety may benefit when they put their own needs first. Parents and other caregivers are better able to offer their children the care and support they require when they are well-rested, well-fed, and emotionally supported. Additionally, parents who take care of themselves may be more likely to teach their children appropriate coping skills, which can foster resilience and emotional control.

Caretakers can help their children manage their anxiety by prioritizing self-care and fostering a positive environment. This can foster a more gratifying and loving relationship between the caregiver and the kid while also easing some of the general stress and responsibilities of caregiving.

It can be difficult and stressful to provide care for a kid with anxiety, but it is crucial for parents to put their own needs first in order to stay healthy and support their child effectively. Caregivers can help their children manage their anxiety by taking steps to manage their own physical and emotional health. This will help them to foster a more encouraging and pleasant atmosphere.

CHAPTER ELEVEN

Case Studies from Managing Stress in Everyday Life

It is always instructive to see examples of how kids and their caregivers navigate this road in real life, despite how much we can read and study about managing anxiety in kids. In this chapter, we'll look at three case studies of anxious kids and the ways in which they and their caregivers deal with it.

1st Case Study Ellie, age 7, suffers from separation anxiety

Ellie, a 7-year-old girl, suffers from excruciating separation anxiety. When her parents are not around, she experiences severe anxiety and struggles to eat, sleep, and attend school. When Ellie was around 4 years old and her mother had to go for business for a few days, Ellie's parents realized that her anxiousness had started. Ellie has since developed a growing anxiety whenever her parents are not present.

After consulting with Ellie's parents, the child psychologist suggested cognitive-behavioral treatment (CBT). Ellie's therapist gradually accustomed her to being away from her parents by using a method known as exposure therapy. The therapist had Ellie practice spending brief periods of time alone in a room while her parents were in another room. The therapist gradually extended Ellie's alone time until she felt at peace being by herself for greater periods of time. In order to create a steady and predictable routine that would make Ellie feels safer, Ellie's therapist also collaborated with her parents.

Case Study 2: Social Anxiety in 10-year-old Jake

Jake, a 10-year-old child with social anxiety, struggles with it. He has a hard time making friends and frequently stays out of social situations. Jake's anxiousness started in first grade after a bad incident he had with a group of peers. Since then, Jake's anxiety in social situations has gotten worse.

A child psychologist who Jake's parents consulted with suggested CBT and social skills instruction. Jake's therapist assisted him in recognizing and challenging any unfavorable ideas he had about social interactions. In order to assist Jake in controlling his anxiety in social situations, his therapist also taught him relaxation techniques including deep breathing and progressive muscle relaxation. Jake's therapist also worked with him on social skills including starting conversations, keeping eye contact, and interpreting body language.

Case Study 3: Generalized Anxiety Disorder in 15-year-old Maya

15-year-old Maya suffers from generalized anxiety disorder. She worries nonstop about a variety of issues, including friends, family, and school. Maya was in middle school when her anxiety first started to affect her, making it difficult for her to complete her homework. Since that time, Maya's anxiety has gotten worse and has started to interfere with her daily activities.

A child psychiatrist who Maya's parents visited with suggested medication and CBT. A selective serotonin reuptake inhibitor (SSRI), a kind of antidepressant that is also useful in treating anxiety, was recommended by Maya's psychiatrist. CBT was utilized by Maya's therapist to assist her in challenging her unfavorable thoughts and assumptions around the issues she was anxious about. In order to assist Maya manage her anxiety, her therapist also worked with her on mindfulness exercises and relaxation methods.

These case studies demonstrate how anxiety can appear in various forms and have an impact on kids of various ages. Additionally, they show that effective methods for controlling anxiety exist, including CBT, social skill development, medication, and relaxation techniques. It is crucial to keep in mind that controlling anxiety is a process that could call for a combination of different tactics and take some time. Children who suffer from anxiety can learn to control their anxiety and grow with the aid of parents, caregivers, mental health specialists, and their schools.

CHAPTER TWELVE

Managing Children's Anxiety during Changes and Transitions

Whenever there is a shift or transition in a child's life, anxiety may occur. Both planned changes—like starting school or moving—and unplanned events—like illness or natural disasters—can cause these adjustments. It is crucial for parents and other adults to know how to support their kids through these situations and assist them in coping with their anxiety.

Techniques for controlling fear of change

Children may experience stress when starting school, moving homes, or switching schools. Here are some tactics that could be useful:

- **Prepare beforehand:** Information regarding the impending shift should be given to your youngster. Show them images of the new place or take them there before the move, for instance, if you are transferring residences. Visit the school and introduce yourself to the teacher if they are starting a new school.

- **Establish a routine:** Creating a routine can give your child comfort and familiarity during a period of adjustment. This can include set mealtimes, bedtimes, and periods for play.

- **Stay upbeat:** Encourage your child to do the same by keeping your attention on the benefits of the transition. Describe the new acquaintances they will make at their new school or the new experiences they will have in their new house, for instance.

- **Listen and validate:** Pay attention and verify Encourage your youngster to communicate their emotions and to share their worries. Let them know that experiencing fear or anxiety during a period of change is normal.

- **Stay engaged:** Keep up contact with your child throughout this time of change. Make time for family activities and go to school events or extracurricular activities with them

Children's coping mechanisms for unforeseen changes

Children may experience trauma from sudden changes, such as illnesses or natural disasters. Here are some tactics that could be useful:

- **Please provide details:** Your child should be given an explanation of the situation that is age- and developmental appropriate. Give them truthful and accurate information, but refrain from giving them too many specifics.

- **Encourage them:** Assure your child that they are secure and that you will take all reasonable precautions to protect them.

- **Make everything seem normal:** As far as you can, try to preserve a sense of routine and normalcy. Bring your child's favorite toys or books, for instance, if they are in the hospital, to create a comfortable atmosphere.

- **Encourage emotional expression:** Encourage your child to share their thoughts about the circumstance. Inform them that it's okay to feel frightened or concerned and that their sentiments are legitimate.

- **Seek assistance:** If necessary, seek assistance from friends, family, or mental health experts. During these trying times, it's crucial to take care of your own mental health.

For kids and their caregivers, coping with anxiety during times of transition and change can be difficult. However, with the correct tools and encouragement, kids can learn to control their anxiety and flourish in these circumstances. To ensure that their children successfully traverse these transitions, parents and other adults who are responsible for them must keep aware, remain actively involved, and ask for help when necessary.

Helen J. Vogt

CHAPTER THIRTEEN

Developing a Healthy Lifestyle in Children to Manage Anxiety

A healthy lifestyle is one of the best methods to lower the risk of anxiety and its symptoms in children and can be fostered through a variety of management techniques. Taking care of oneself physically, mentally, and emotionally is part of living a healthy lifestyle. Healthy behaviors in childhood increase the likelihood of greater mental and physical health, which can aid in better anxiety and stress management. The association between lifestyle factors and childhood anxiety will be covered in this chapter, along with methods for encouraging a healthy lifestyle.

The connection between lifestyle elements and children's anxiety

In addition to being crucial for overall health, lifestyle factors like nutrition, exercise, and sleep can have a big impact on how anxious kids are.

A nutrient-rich, less processed diet can elevate mood and lessen signs of anxiety. A Mediterranean-style diet, which places an emphasis on whole grains, fruits, vegetables, lean protein, and healthy fats, has been linked to decreased levels of anxiety in both adults and children, according to studies. A diet heavy in processed foods and sweets, however, can worsen the body's inflammatory levels, which can heighten anxiety.

Another crucial lifestyle element that can assist in managing children's anxiety is exercise. By increasing the release of endorphins, the brain's feel-good chemicals, regular exercise can lower stress and elevate mood. Additionally, exercise can enhance the quality of sleep, which is crucial for emotional health and can lessen the symptoms of anxiety. Children who participate in regular physical activity are less likely to experience anxiety and depression, according to studies.

For both physical and mental well-being, sleep is essential. Lack of sleep increases a child's risk of developing anxiety and other emotional issues. Lack of sleep can cause irritation, mood changes, and difficulties concentrating, all of which can aggravate the symptoms of anxiety. Better sleep hygiene in children can be encouraged by establishing a regular bedtime routine and establishing a relaxing bedroom atmosphere.

How to Manage Anxiety by Promoting a Healthy Lifestyle

Encourage Healthy Eating Habits: By providing a range of nutritious foods including fruits, vegetables, lean protein, and whole grains, parents can encourage healthy eating habits in their children. Limiting processed and sugary foods can also assist to lower bodily inflammation and ease the feelings of anxiety. To promote healthy eating habits, parents can get their kids involved in the meal planning and preparation process.

Encourage Children to Exercise Regularly: Parents can encourage their kids to exercise regularly by giving them opportunities for active play, getting involved in sports or other physical activities, and encouraging outside play. Daily activities like biking or walking to school are excellent ways to fit exercise into your schedule.

Establish a Regular Sleep Routine: By establishing a regular bedtime and wake-up time, developing a relaxing bedtime routine, and creating a cozy sleeping environment, parents may help their children develop a regular sleep routine. Better sleep hygiene in kids can also be encouraged by limiting screen time before bed and avoiding caffeine in the late afternoon and evening.

Encourage Mindfulness and Relaxation Methods: By lowering stress levels and fostering a sense of calm, mindfulness and relaxation methods, such as yoga, deep breathing, and meditation, can help kids manage their anxiety. Parents can support these behaviors by serving as role models and incorporating them into regular activities.

Provide Opportunities for Social Support: Creating opportunities for social support is crucial for mental well-being and can help with the symptoms of anxiety. Children can be given the chance to participate in social activities like play dates or sports teams, and parents can promote honest conversation about feelings and emotions.

Make Your Home a calm Place: Children's anxiety levels can be decreased by fostering a serene and encouraging home environment. By setting routines, offering a secure and comfortable home, and limiting their children's exposure to stresses like excessive screen time and the news, parents can help their children feel calm.

Developing a healthy lifestyle in kids is essential to reducing anxiety and fostering general wellbeing. Children can manage anxiety by practicing good dietary practices, encouraging regular exercise, developing regular sleep schedules, encouraging mindfulness and relaxation techniques, offering chances for social support, and maintaining a quiet home atmosphere.

CHAPTER FOURTEEN

Providing Support for Kids with Co-Occurring Conditions

It can be challenging to treat and manage children with anxiety because co-occurring disorders are common in this population. ADHD, depression, and substance use disorders are some of the most often encountered co-occurring problems. It is crucial to comprehend how anxiety and related illnesses interact for children to receive supportive care that works.

Anxiety and Co-Occurring Conditions: Relationship

According to some research, up to 50% of children with ADHD also experience anxiety. Anxiety and ADHD frequently co-occur. Worry, fear, and avoidance are just a few of the anxiety symptoms that can have an impact on social relationships and academic performance, which can make ADHD symptoms worse. In addition to having concentration and focus issues, children with anxiety and

ADHD may also exhibit increased impulsivity and hyperactivity. To provide the child the best results, it is crucial to recognize and treat both diseases at once.

Another frequent ailment that coexists with anxiety in youngsters is depression. Constant worry and fear, among other anxiety-related symptoms, can result in depressive symptoms of hopelessness and helplessness. Children who experience both anxiety and depression may have trouble concentrating, sleeping, and eating. Also possible for them are feelings of exhaustion and a lack of motivation. Work with a mental health expert to create an effective treatment plan. Cognitive-behavioral therapy and medication may be used to address both disorders.

Children with anxiety should also be concerned about substance use disorders. Anxiety can cause self-medication with alcohol or drugs, which can worsen symptoms and result in addiction. A comprehensive treatment strategy that concurrently treats both diseases is required for children with anxiety and substance use disorders. This may entail behavioral therapy, family support, and medication-assisted treatment.

Supporting Children with Co-Occurring Conditions: Strategies

An integrated strategy that treats both anxiety and co-occurring disorder is the most efficient course of therapy for kids with co-occurring conditions. A mix of medication, therapy, and lifestyle modifications may be necessary. Here are some methods for helping kids with co-occurring conditions:

- **Look for expert assistance:** Creating a successful treatment plan requires collaboration with a mental health specialist who specializes in treating co-occurring illnesses. A mental health expert can assist in determining the child's best course of treatment.

- **Use treatments that are backed by evidence:** Both anxiety and depression can be effectively treated with cognitive-behavioral therapy. The treatment of anxiety and co-occurring disorders may also be appropriate with medication.

- **Promote adjustments to a healthy lifestyle:** Promoting healthy lifestyle modifications like consistent exercise, a nutritious diet, and sufficient sleep can help lessen the symptoms of anxiety and other co-occurring illnesses.

- **Offer family support:** For kids with co-occurring disorders, family support is crucial. Parents and other caregivers should become knowledgeable about the condition of the kid and acquire skills for offering assistance and controlling symptoms.

- **Monitor progress:** Follow up on the child's progress frequently to make sure the treatment is having the desired effect. The child's mental health practitioner should be informed of any concerns, and parents and caregivers should keep track of symptoms.

Children with anxiety frequently have co-occurring illnesses, which can make treatment and management more challenging. It is crucial to comprehend how anxiety and other illnesses interact for adults to effectively support children. The best treatment is a holistic strategy that tackles both anxiety and the co-occurring disorder. Supporting children with co-occurring conditions involves seeking professional assistance, putting evidence-based therapies into practice, encouraging healthy lifestyle changes, offering family support, and keeping track of progress. Children with co-occurring illnesses can learn to control their symptoms and have healthy, full lives with the right support and treatment.

CHAPTER FIFTEEN

Navigating the Road to Managing Children's Anxiety

Children's anxiety management is a path that calls for dedication, endurance, and constant support. It is crucial to have a plan in place for continuing progress and handling setbacks as well as to seek expert assistance when necessary.

Getting Professional Assistance

It's crucial to get medical assistance if your child is experiencing anxiety. A physician, a school counselor, or a mental health specialist like a psychologist or psychiatrist may fall under this category. To assist children manage their anxiety, these professionals can offer evaluations, diagnoses, and evidence-based therapies.

Finding a specialist with experience working with children and a specialty in treating anxiety is crucial when looking for professional assistance. Asking for recommendations from dependable people, such your child's pediatrician or school counselor, as well as doing online research on potential providers, may be beneficial.

Ongoing Assistance

Children who are anxious need constant support. This can entail frequent therapy sessions, check-ups with a pediatrician, and dialogue with educators. It's crucial to maintain an open line of communication with your kid about their worry and to offer encouragement and acceptance while they deal with their symptoms.

Continuous help like that provided by support groups or counseling, may also be advantageous for parents and carers. It can be challenging to control a child's anxiety, so it's crucial to look after your own wellbeing.

Keeping Ahead of Reversals and Managing Progress

Children's anxiety management is not usually a straightforward process. Even if there can be obstacles or setbacks along the way, it's crucial to stick with the plan and keep moving forward. This could entail keeping up with therapy or medication, engaging in self-care and coping mechanisms, and giving your child continual support.

It's crucial to have a strategy in place for dealing with setbacks. This can entail developing a crisis plan or knowing when to take your child to the hospital in case of an urgent anxiety attack. You may feel more assured in your abilities to control your child's anxiety if you have a plan in place.

Children's anxiety management is a path that calls for dedication, endurance, and constant support. A crucial part of this journey is seeking expert assistance, offering continuing support, and having a strategy in place for handling setbacks. Children with anxiety can learn to control their symptoms and thrive with the correct resources and assistance.

CONCLUSION

In conclusion, anxiety affects a lot of kids' mental health and has a big impact on their everyday lives and general wellbeing. But kids can learn to control their fear and build resilience with the correct help and treatments. Understanding anxiety, encouraging emotional control and resilience, and supporting kids with co-occurring illnesses are just a few of the themes covered in this book's discussion on how to manage anxiety in kids.

The importance of parents and other adult caregivers in fostering children's emotional wellbeing is one thing readers should take away from this book. Caregivers can support children in learning the coping mechanisms necessary to handle anxiety by creating a safe and nurturing environment. This includes fostering a healthy lifestyle, such as balanced nutrition, regular exercise, and adequate sleep, as well as knowing the various personality types and age-specific anxiety management techniques.

The significance of getting expert assistance when required is another important lesson to learn. While parents can offer a lot of support, some kids might also require extra interventions, such cognitive-behavioral therapy or medication, to effectively manage their anxiety. Working with a skilled mental health practitioner who can offer direction and support during the therapy process is crucial in these situations.

In general, treating anxiety in children necessitates a thorough and diverse strategy that takes into accounts each child's particular requirements and environment. The information in this book can assist parents, guardians, and mental health professionals in supporting children in controlling their anxiety, encouraging resilience, and leading happy lives. Together, we can assist kids in overcoming their anxiety and acquiring the abilities they need to flourish.